For Ben – C.H.

For Mum and Dad, with love – C.W.

First published in 1994 by Magi Publications
55 Crowland Avenue, Hayes, Middlesex UB3 4JP

This edition published in 1995

Text © 1994 by Christine Harris
Illustrations © 1994 by Catherine Walters

The right of Christine Harris to be identified as the author
of this work has been asserted by her in accordance with
The Copyright, Designs and Patents Act 1988.

Printed and bound in Belgium by Proost N.V. Turnhout

ISBN 1 85430 129 2

Oliver All Alone

MAGI PUBLICATIONS

Oliver All Alone

by **Christine Harris**

illustrated by **Catherine Walters**

MAGI PUBLICATIONS

London

Gemma

Oliver stood in the hall with his lead in his mouth.

"They're not leaving without me?" he said. "They *never* leave without me. I'm too little to be left in the house all alone."

"Sorry, Oliver," said Mum. "As it's Christmas Eve, we're taking presents to Gran in hospital, and puppies aren't allowed there. Never mind, we shan't be long."

Oliver heard the *crunch-crunch* of footsteps in the snow, and the slam of the car doors.

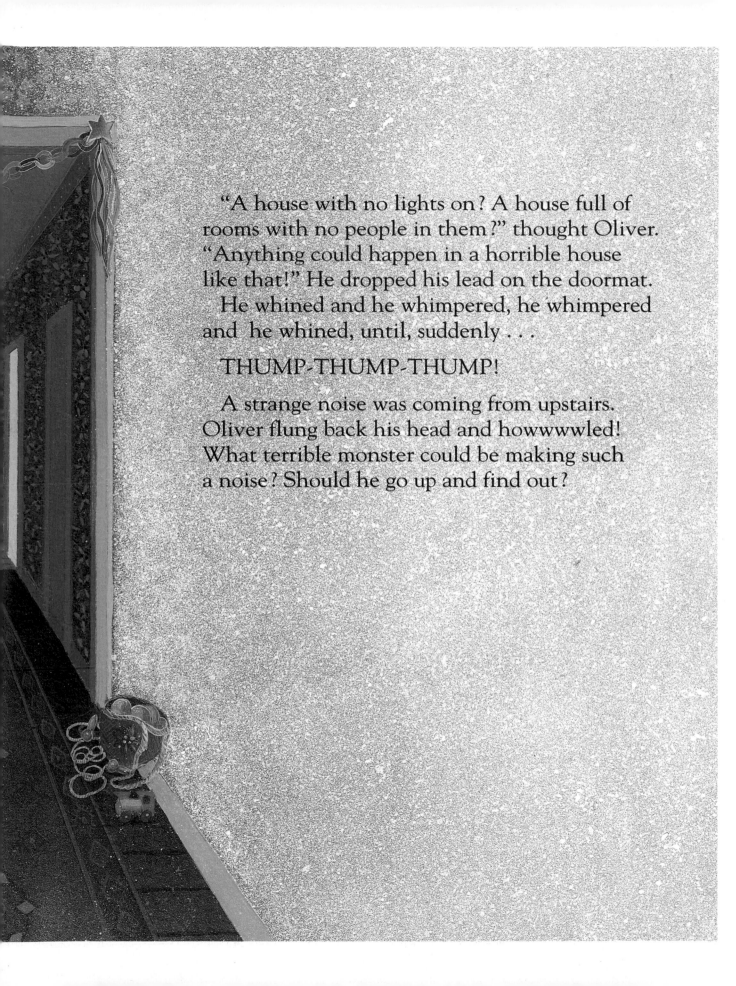

"A house with no lights on? A house full of rooms with no people in them?" thought Oliver. "Anything could happen in a horrible house like that!" He dropped his lead on the doormat.

He whined and he whimpered, he whimpered and he whined, until, suddenly . . .

THUMP-THUMP-THUMP!

A strange noise was coming from upstairs. Oliver flung back his head and howwwwled! What terrible monster could be making such a noise? Should he go up and find out?

Oliver crept upstairs, and crawled along the landing with his tummy close to the carpet. He peered into Mum's and Dad's bedroom. That beastly, bulging, stringy-tailed shape on the bed – was *that* the monster?

"Grrh, I'm coming to get you," growled Oliver.
He launched into battle against the stringy-tailed monster.
He snarled and chewed, he chewed and snarled.
But then he pricked up his ears.

THUMP-THUMP-THUMP!

The monster was making noises, but from somewhere else!
Had the monster escaped?

Oliver raced across to the window, stood on his hind legs, and looked out.

Could that be the monster? That white ghostly thing half-way down the garden?

"Come inside and let me get at you," yelped Oliver.
He scrabbled and scratched at the window.
But the white ghostly thing refused to answer him.
"You're scared, scared, SCARED!"
Oliver was making such a noise, he almost didn't hear it.

THUMP-THUMP-THUMP!

But where was it coming from?
Somewhere behind him!

"My blanket's in the kitchen," thought Oliver. "I'll hide under it in my basket, so the monster won't be able to find me."

He crept downstairs and, as fast as his plump puppy legs could carry him, he skedaddled into the kitchen – and braked to a sudden halt.

There was a huge lumpy shape squatting on the kitchen table!

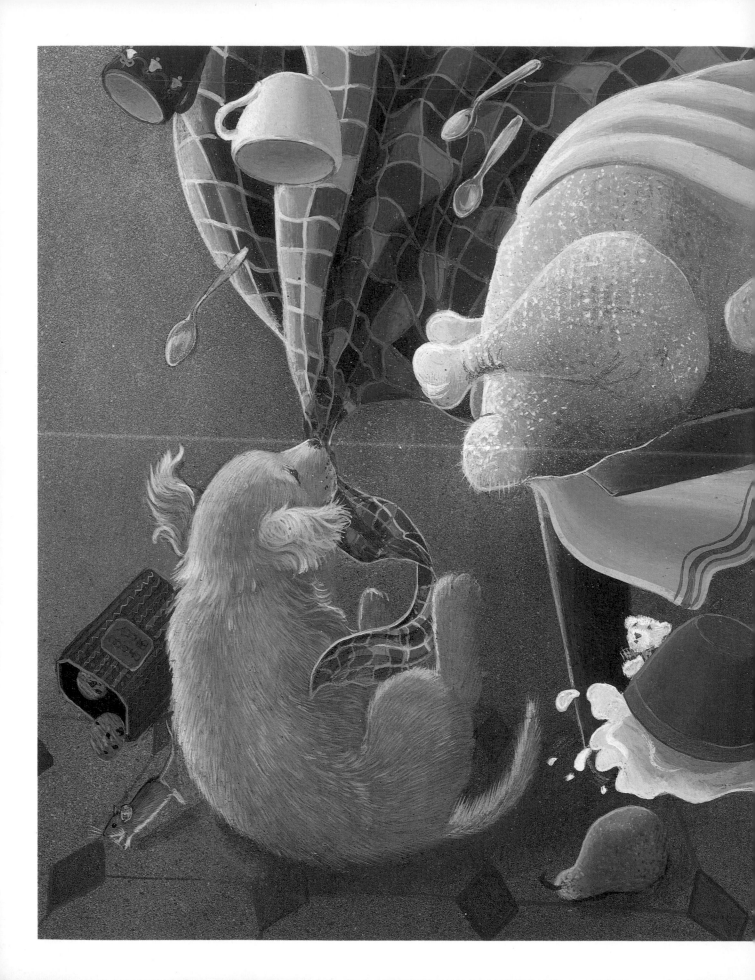

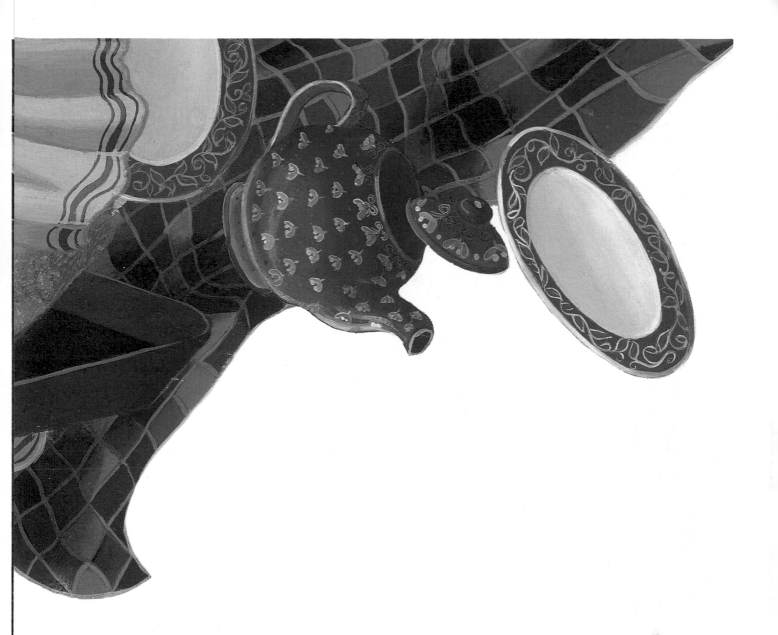

"I'll pull it off the table," thought Oliver. "Then it can't spring on top of me."

He seized one end of the tablecloth, and the lumpy shape came crashing to the floor.

"Fight me if you dare," he barked, butting the shape with his nose. Its skin was cold as ice and as hard as iron. What sort of monster felt like that?

And why could he hear another THUMP-THUMP-THUMP, coming from the sitting room?

"Wake up and fight!" yapped Oliver, as he sprang towards it. He head-butted the sleeping monster so that it fell sideways with its mouth wide open. Would it swallow him whole? Now he was fighting the monster's slippery, glittery tentacles. He struggled free.

THUMP-THUMP-THUMP!

Oh, no! That noise again – and this time it was coming from the dining room!

Suppose when Mum and Dad and the children came home the THUMP-THUMP-THUMP Monster leapt out at them?

"I can't let that happen," thought Oliver.

He inched towards the dining room door.

He had caught up with the monster at last!

He could see the strange shape of its shadow on the wall!

And there in the dining room . . .

. . . was a man, not a monster at all! A nice smiling man in a red coat.

"I'm a bit early tonight," he said. "Everyone is still out, except you. Were you left to guard the house then? And now you've found me. Well, here's your reward for being so clever and brave. A Christmas bone! And a little present for your teddy."

Just then, Oliver heard the front door open . . .